One afternoon,
Chirri and Chirra play in the
meadow in front of their house.

Kaya Doi

Chirri & Chirra
In the Tall Grass

Translated from the Japanese by
Yuki Kaneko

ENCHANTED LION BOOKS
NEW YORK

Dring-dring, dring-dring!
Chirri and Chirra pedal
through the tall grass.

When they come out of
the grass, gigantic white
clover surprise them.

A bumblebee comes
and collects honey.

Dring-dring, dring-dring!
Chirri and Chirra follow the bumblebee.

They arrive at the
bumblebee's house.

Chirri and Chirra peek inside and see many kinds of honey.

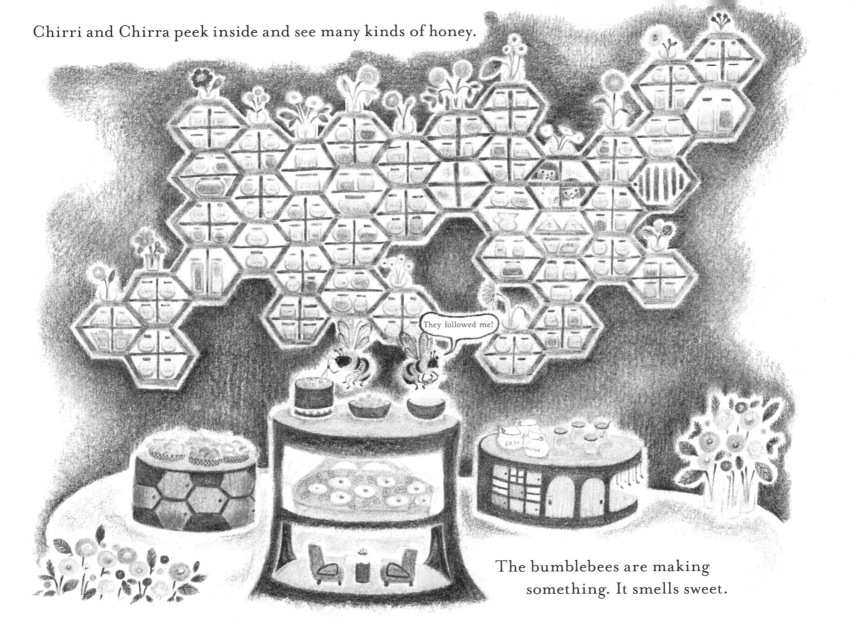

The bumblebees are making something. It smells sweet.

They've just made honey
sponge cake balls wrapped
in flower petals.

The bumblebees share the cakes with
Chirri and Chirra, who enjoy them under
a flowering hydrangea bush.

A pair of flower chafers come
and take a hydrangea leaf.

Dring–dring, dring–dring!
Chirri and Chirra follow
the flower chafers.

They arrive at the flower chafers' house.
Chirri and Chirra peek inside and see all sorts of leaves.

The flower chafers are making something.

It smells so fresh!

They've just made freshly
squeezed mixed-leaf juice,
with yumberry fruit and
raspberry pulp.

They pour glasses of fresh juice
for Chirri and Chirra,
who enjoy their drinks on
a warm rock.

A lizard passes in front of them.

Dring-dring, dring-dring!
Chirri and Chirra follow the lizard.

They arrive
at the lizard's house.

Chirri and Chirra peek inside.

"Please come in and give me a hand,"
  says the lizard.

The lizard's house is made of fluorite
that sparkles with many colors.
Chirri and Chirra are
happy to help.

They melt shards of the crystal in a pot, adding leaf juice and honey. Then they pour the mixture into molds to cool and set.

They have made fluorite candies!

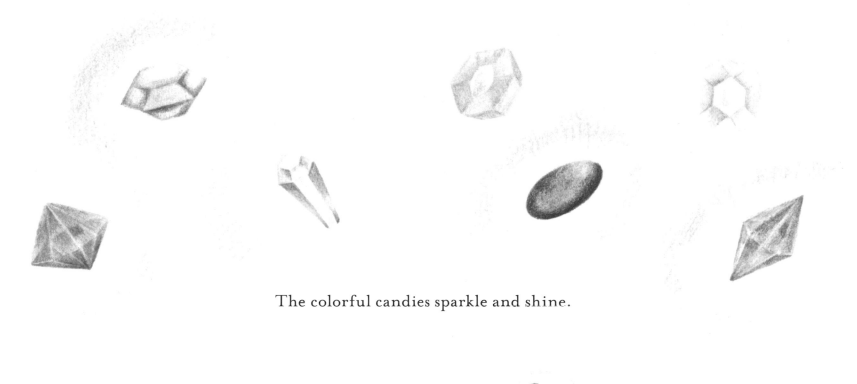

The colorful candies sparkle and shine.

Some fireflies arrive.
Each gets a freshly made candy and
flies away.

It's beginning to get dark outside.
Chirri and Chirra each get a candy for the ride home.

Dring-dring, dring-dring!
Chirri and Chirra enjoy their candies
as they pedal along.

The fireflies light
up a path through
the tall grass.

Dring-dring, dring-dring!
When Chirri and Chirra come out of the grass,
their candies go *poof!* and disappear.

Dring–dring, dring–dring!
A lovely dusk falls over the meadow.

Born in Tokyo, Kaya Doi graduated with a degree in design from Tokyo Zokei University.
She got her start in picture books by attending the Atosaki Juku Workshop, a program at a Tokyo bookshop.
Prolific and popular, Doi has created many wonderful books. She now lives in Chiba Prefecture
and maintains a strong interest in environmental and animal welfare issues.

www.enchantedlion.com

First edition, published in 2017 by Enchanted Lion Books,
67 West Street, 317A, Brooklyn, NY 11222
Text and illustrations copyright © 2007 by Kaya Doi.
English translation rights arranged with Alice-kan Ltd. through Japan UNI Agency, Inc.
All rights reserved under International and Pan-American Copyright Conventions.
A CIP record is on file with the Library of Congress. ISBN 978-1-59270-225-1
Printed in China in January 2017 by RR Donnelley Asia Printing Solutions Ltd.
1 3 5 7 9 10 8 6 4 2